Celebrating

Dragon Boat Festival

Copyright © 2007 Shanghai Press and Publishing Development Company

This book is edited and design̶e̶d̶ ̶b̶y̶ ̶t̶h̶e̶ Editorial Committee of *Cultural China* series

Managing Directors: Wa̶n̶g̶ ̶Y̶o̶u̶, Xu Naiqing
Editorial Director: ̶W̶u̶ Ying
Editor: Yang Xiaohe

Story and Illustrations: Sanmu Tang
Translation: Mina Tenison

ISBN-13: 978-1-60220-968-8

Address any comments about *Celebrating the Dragon Boat Festival* to:

Better Link Press
99 Park Ave
New York, NY 10016
USA
or
Shanghai Press and Publishing Development Company
F 7 Donghu Road, Shanghai, China (200031)
Email: comments_betterlinkpress@hotmail.com

Computer typeset by Sanmu Tang
Printed in China by Shanghai Donnelley Printing Co. Ltd.

1   2   3   4   5   6   7   8   9   10

Celebrating the Dragon Boat Festival

By Sanmu Tang

Better Link Press

Today must be a very special day. In the morning, Dad hung some herbs on the front gate, and granny put a scented pouch around my neck. It had a strange and wonderful smell.

And Mum bought something I've never seen before
— weird green leaves.

She also put a whole week's of rice in a tub of water.

"What is happening today? Is this a special day, Granny?"

"Yes, Little Mei. Today is the fifth day of the fifth month in
the lunar year. We call it the Dragon Boat Festival.
On the door we hang traditional herbs and we carry
a scented pouch on our bodies to ward off evil spirits."

"And why is Mommy putting so much rice in the water?"

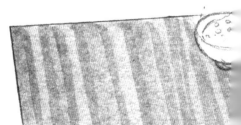

"Mum is preparing to make *zongzi*, sticky rice balls wrapped in the leaves of reeds. This is the most important food to prepare for the Dragon Boat Festival."

How to make *zongzi*

1. Soak some sticky rice in water for 3 hours until it is soft.

2. Soak the leaves in water to keep them wet and fresh.

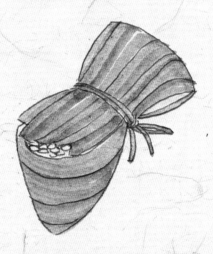

5. Use a string to tightly wrap the *zongzi*.

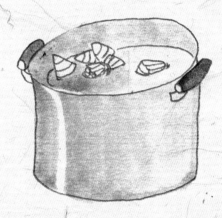

6. Put the *zongzi* in water boiling to cook.

4. Line up two leaves side by side, overlapping slightly to make them wide enough to fold the leaves into a pyramid shape. Place the sticky rice and the filling inside and continue to fold the leaves over several times.

3. Prepare the meat, red bean paste, jujube paste, and other materials to make the filling for the rice.

7. Using the lowest heat, simmer the *zongzi* for 5-6 hours.

8. The *zongzi* is now ready to eat.

"Why must we use leaves to wrap up the filling?

Isn't it too much trouble?"

"Go ask Grandpa. He will tell you the story behind it."

"More than two thousand years ago in the Kingdom of Chu lived a patriotic poet named Qu Yuan. He discovered that the neighboring Kingdom of Qin wanted to conquer the Kingdom of Chu. He immediately told the King of Chu, who refused to believe him and banished him instead."

Several years later, the capital of Chu was attacked and taken by the Qin. When Qu Yuan received the news, he fell in despair and tossed himself into the Miluo River.

When the people found out, they were terribly sad. They rowed their boats up and down to rescue Qu Yuan, but could not find him. Then the people began to toss rice balls as sacrifices to Qu Yuan. To make sure that the fish could not steal the rice, they wrapped the rice in reed leaves. And that is why we eat *zongzi* during the Dragon Boat Festival.

"Grandpa, Dad, the *zongzi* is ready now!"

"It smells delicious."

"Do you know how to eat it, Little Mei?
First, unwrap the strings. Then slowly open
up the leaves and put the sticky rice on a
plate. Now you can use your chopsticks to eat it.
"Wow! So many different flavors!"

"Little Mei, would you like to go to the river to see the Dragon Boat festivities?"

"Right now? Yes, please let's go! I can't wait!"

"Wow, look at the dragon boats!
They have so many colors."

"Look, everyone is rowing so fast!"

Little Mei now knows why we celebrate the Dragon Boat Festival.